**What readers are saying about** *Plain Revenge*

"For anyone who is curious about the Amish, this book is a great way to learn more about the culture while enjoying a short story. If you have lived in or visited Lancaster on a vacation, you will find familiar places that really help you visualize and enjoy the story!"

"It was an easy, one evening read, and I didnt want to put it down. I like that the author put facts about the Amish throughout the book."

"Learned a lot about the Amish people which surprised me. Great short story."

"I liked the history posts about the Amish and learned a lot. I live near Amish and found them to be very accurate. The story was intriguing - suspenseful without being too gory. I do want to find this 'Hatchet Man's mill.'"

# Plain

# Revenge

A short story taken from
Lancaster County

Brian K. Fulmer

## Acknowledgments

I want to thank the current Strasburg chief of police, Steve Echternach, for his input throughout this process. Thank you to Jill Reichert and Diane Omondi for editing. Thank you to my Amish friends for input and adjustments to the "Amish" portions. Thank you to Katie Lapp for translating Pennsylvania Dutch. Apologies to my wife Laurie who now worries about Amish buggies when she hears them late at night!

## Dedication

This story is dedicated to all my friends who spent many nights scaring people at Hatchet Man's. I have fond memories!

# Authors Note

I have lived in or around Strasburg Pennsylvania for the majority of my life. Strasburg was my favorite hangout town during my High School years. There really was an abandoned mill that we called "Hatchet Man's" back then. Since that time it has been beautifully renovated into a home where friends of mine live. The description in this story is how I remember that place, not the way it looks today! I changed (or moved) many of the roads in the story. The road names and other geographic descriptions are true but I took many liberties in making them fit. Sadly, I watched the bowling alley burn down several years ago. I kept it in the story for nostalgic reasons.

The Amish are members of the Christian faith with German Swiss Anabaptist history. Anabaptist faith requires adult baptism in a public declaration of faith rather than infant baptism. Believers also avoid military involvement and strive to lead a peaceful non-violent life. Amish are known for their plain dress, simple lifestyle and rejection of modern technology. There are approximately 300,000 Amish in the United States and Canada with the highest populations in Pennsylvania, Ohio and Indiana. Amish speak a dialect of German that is called Pennsylvania Dutch. Church membership begins with baptism, usually between the ages of sixteen and twenty-five. Church membership is a requirement for marriage and members may only marry within the church. Nearly ninety percent of Amish teenagers choose to be baptized and join the church. Those who do not join the church may continue relating with family and friends, but these relationships will be limited and restricted. Consequences of not joining the church vary in different groupings among the Amish.

# Plain
# Revenge

**June 2013 Holmes County Ohio, County Prison**

A series of prison doors opened and closed, each resonating with a desolate clang. As the final door opened into the lobby, the prisoner could see freedom for the first time in three years. A guard escorted the prisoner out of the prison and into a taxi that was waiting outside the gate. Their good-bye sentiments were short. The now former prisoner got into the car with only the clothes on his back and a few toiletries. Another chapter in a volatile life came to a close and an even more volatile chapter was about to begin.

**Sunday, July 2014, Holmes County, Ohio**

Four Amish teenage girls walked side-by-side bare-foot along a winding, rural farm road. Their dark dresses did little to warn passing drivers that they were on the road. Walking four abreast could have made it difficult for a vehicle to pass. The car approaching from behind did not coax the girls to move off the road. Instead, it sped undaunted into their informal line-up. Admittedly, a driver with headlights on at dusk may not have seen them in time to avoid hitting them.

The impact sent all four girls flying in different directions. Two of the girls, Katie, age 16, and Sarah, age 15, were killed instantly. Grace, age 16, was badly injured and died in the hospital. Emma, age 16, survived but faced a long journey of rehabilitation ahead.

No one saw the car that hit the girls. It was nearly a mile between the farm they had left and the farm where they were going. The incident was declared a "hit and run, vehicular homicide" and the police in the surrounding counties started hunting down the driver. They never found him. At that hour of the evening, it could have been understood as a terrible accident. But he had driven off, making it only worse. Never finding the driver made it unforgivable.

## Sunday night, 11:30 P.M., June 14 2015, Strasburg Township, Lancaster County Pennsylvania

John and Mary Leaman had just finished watching the Phillies lose to the San Francisco Giants in a late west coast game. Mary was in bed trying to get to sleep and heard the familiar clip-clop, clip-clop of Amish buggies going by their home on Bunker Hill Road. It was a quiet, early summer night, warm enough to sleep with windows open. Mary could hear the sound of young Amish teens going home from their social gatherings. The Leamans lived in a modest 1960s three-bedroom, stone rancher that was bordered by four similar homes that were built on road frontage. Behind the five houses were fifty acres of prime Lancaster County farmland that were farmed by Old Order Amish families. Corn was planted in the rich soil, and in two more months it would be seven feet tall, blocking any view from the rear of the Leaman house.

Neither John nor Mary thought much about the gunfire they heard in the distance. Like the sound of buggies on the road, gunfire at night was not strange in rural Strasburg. It was probably just a farmer shooting at a stray animal.

Fall communion takes place the Sunday after Fast Day on October 11. At the end of the church service, the names of the girls and who they are planning to marry are announced. At home, many ceremonies and activities are carried out as a way of uniting the two families, including the bride making a meal for her future in-laws.

Amish weddings generally take place on Tuesdays and Thursdays in November. This is after the harvest work is done and before the hard winter sets in. It is not uncommon for Amish businesses to be closed on these days so that everyone can take part in the wedding celebrations.

A blue dress is often the color of choice for brides. The bride has also likely made her own dress which is unadorned, with no fancy trim. This dress will also be worn again for Sunday church, and she may be buried in it at her funeral. There are no flowers at the wedding, and the bride will wear a black prayer covering instead of the normal white veil. The groom and his men will wear all-black suits with hooks and eyes but no buttons. Amish couples do not go away for romantic honeymoons. Their first night of marriage is spent at the bride's house so that she can get up early and help with cleaning the house after the previous day's celebration. The remainder of the honeymoon is spent visiting relatives and collecting practical wedding gifts. The newlywed couple will continue living with the bride's parents until spring, when they set up their own home.

Amos Zook and Lydia Beiler were a courting Amish couple with plans to marry at the set time in November after the harvest season. They rounded a sharp corner on Bunker Hill Road and the wheels of their open courting buggy slid off the pavement onto the stone shoulder. Amos cracked the reigns of the horse and the buggy pulled back up to the smoother surface. The moon was shining and the air was cool. The couple was in love and they were sitting against each other with a blanket over them to stay warm during the five mile trip home after a night out with friends. They had just split off from a three-buggy caravan and were now traveling alone on a narrow, lightly traveled road that led to Mary's farm on Deiter Road.

The road was bumpy and Amos tried to avoid the worst holes. A mile from Lydia's home there was an out-cropping of limestone rocks that had been quarried some years ago. There were a few trees and a small pond where the Amish children ice skated when the pond froze over in the winter. They didn't notice the movement behind the rocks, nor did they hear the gunfire that cracked through the quiet of the night. Two shots were fired.

Amos and Lydia were hit in the chest within seconds of each other. Neither knew what hit them. The force of the bullets slammed them back on the padded seat, and they both slumped down and fell to the floor of the buggy with their blood pooling beneath them. The night returned quiet except for the sound of the horse pulling the buggy along in a frightened trot on the rough pavement. The horse knew where it was going, and continued its journey to Lydia's farm. There it stopped.

Amish courtship traditionally begins at age sixteen for the boys and age fourteen to fifteen for the girls. In order to find someone to date, the young people need to join an active youth group. The Amish socialize at functions like visits, frolics, and church. Since Amish only go to church every other week, it makes sense for the older kids to stay late after church to mix and match. Sunday activities include volleyball matches and other outside games. In the evenings, the youth will meet in the same house as church for Sunday night singing. The Sunday night singing is not meant for devotion. The songs of worship are faster and more energetic than the slowly chanted songs of the morning church service.

The boys and girls sit at a long table facing each other. There is plenty of time between songs to talk and socialize. The singing lasts until around ten o'clock p.m. The group will then hang around for an hour or two after singing, with the unattached boys and girls sizing each other up in a search for likely partners. If a couple hits it off, the Amish dating process begins with the boy asking the girl if he can drive her home. At her house they will go in and visit. At that late hour, the household will be sleeping so they have plenty of privacy. They may sit up long into the night getting to know each other. The boy makes the long buggy trip home in the wee hours of the morning. If both are willing, the couple starts going steady.

Amish meet for church every other weekend. On the weekend when there is no church, the couple usually dates on Saturday night. That way they can see each other every week. Either party can quit the relationship at any time. Just as in the outside world, it might take someone several tries to find a lifelong partner. The more conservative couples practice traditional Amish dating customs. They date in their buggies and drink hot chocolate or sodas. They focus on group and outdoor activities, sometimes with their parents.

Lydia's father, Mervin, walked out of his house at 4:30 a.m. to milk his eighty Holstein cows. His wife, Ida, was still inside getting ready to help with the farm chores before returning to make breakfast at six o'clock. Mervin saw the horse and buggy in the driveway and wandered over to see why it had stopped there. He was not prepared for the scene that awaited him. He found his daughter and Amos slumped over in the buggy. He shouted to his wife Ida, "Kum raus! Gruat na! Shnell!" in Pennsylvania Dutch meaning to come out immediately.

At the same time he ran to the small booth-type structure in the yard to call for an ambulance. Amish phones are often in small out-buildings or in the barn so they do not violate the church rules that prohibit having a phone in the house. Mervin quickly called 911 and reported what he had seen before running back to his wife who stood in shock beside the open carriage.

Sirens were heard coming from three miles away in Strasburg. Since the Beiler's lived outside of the Borough of Strasburg, they fell into the jurisdiction of the Pennsylvania State Police. The first trooper arrived in ten minutes, right behind an ambulance. Upon the officer's first assessment, she immediately put out a call for backup and homicide detectives. The ambulance crew checked for vital signs on the two victims, but it was clear that their lives had already ended. A fire rescue squad pulled up to the property but there was little they could do except set up road blocks and direct traffic away from the scene.

Within an hour, the normally quiet farm was swarming with State troopers, detectives, local Strasburg police, fire police and reporters. Horrified Amish neighbors and family were coming from every direction and stood together at the edge of the yard. Buggies lined the road in both directions leading up to the farm; it was a struggle for the fire police and troopers to keep everyone out of the crime scene. A State Police helicopter circled above the area scanning for any movement or suspicious activity.

Mervin Beiler had been quick to disconnect the agitated horse from the buggy before the police arrived because he was afraid the horse would get spooked by all the strangers. But apart from that, everything else was left untouched for the police. A police photographer took pictures of the buggy and two bodies; an investigator began to analyze what he could see.

The area around the buggy was taped off and only the officials were permitted to approach the scene. The local fire police struggled to keep onlookers from getting near the property. After the medical examiner checked the victims and took more pictures, he and his team carefully put the bodies into body bags and moved them into a van for transport to the county morgue. The autopsies to be done at the morgue would include taking fingerprints and blood samples, as well as documenting body markings.

There were no surprises in any of the tests. The gunshot wounds went straight through – entry into the chest and exit from the back. It was evident that the two were killed while sitting in the buggy and then slumped to the floor and to their death. Evidence showed that Amos and Lydia had not been killed elsewhere and then their bodies relocated to the buggy. The time of death was between 12:00 a.m. and 1:00 a.m., and they had not been moved after death. From the trajectory of the bullet wounds, the examiner concluded the shooter was slightly elevated — maybe three to four feet — which would have allowed the shooter to miss the horse and land his bullets on the unsuspecting couple.

*******************

Inside the farmhouse, Detective Sanchez and Chief Miller sat on a long backless bench at a picnic-style kitchen table with four grieving parents who could not understand how anyone could do this to their children. Chief Miller asked everyone to gather hands and pray for Divine guidance and strength. "Hemlich Vadda, meah commha tsu deich dah miya. Meah froah fa diy schonung un gnaudy tsu de lat un edah kinnah es um vey du sin. Dear Father God, we come to you today and ask for your mercy and grace to these hurting families."

Detective Sanchez looked at Miller in shock. It wasn't clear if his surprise was because the Chief had prayed with the victims, or because he said the prayer in Pennsylvania Dutch.

Chief Miller introduced Sanchez to those who were gathered: Abram and Fannie Zook, parents of Amos, Mervin and Ida Beiler, parents of Lydia, three grandparents and a number of siblings. He offered the family members his condolences in Dutch, then explained the police procedures and introduced Detective Sanchez. After going that far in Pennsylvania Dutch, he asked permission to carry on in English so that Sanchez could participate in the conversation. With the consent of the family, Chief Miller told Sanchez, "Go ahead. They can communicate in English; they are just more comfortable with Dutch." By that time, Sanchez looked like he was in another world.

The farm house had a very basic interior. The floors were stained wood with very old linoleum in the kitchen area. There was a propane lamp in the corner, lighting the room and giving off a sickly oil vapor that made Sanchez feel sick. The house was old, with fading wallpaper on the walls and dark green shades on the windows. It was functional for a large family, but held little aesthetic appeal.

Sanchez spoke gently to the families, "I am sorry for your loss. We will do everything in our power to find what happened to your children and arrest and punish the person or persons who did this."

Then Abram Zook spoke up. "Mr. Sanchez, we are God-fearing and forgiving people. Whoever did this will face God's judgment. We are not looking for any revenge."

Chief Miller replied, "Mr. Zook, I understand your feelings but we are not seeking revenge either. Our job is to find those who are responsible and stop them from hurting anyone else."

Sanchez continued by asking Lydia's father, "When did you find the buggy with Amos and Lydia?"

Mervin replied slowly, "I saw the horse and buggy at 4:30 this morning when I went to milk the cows. The buggy is still sitting in the same spot it was then. I went to the buggy to see if anyone was inside. There were the two bodies, Amos and our daughter, slumped over on the floor. When I saw the blood, I shouted for my wife to come, and I ran to call the police. I unhooked the horse because she was upset and stomping her hooves. I was afraid she was going to run off."

"Did you touch the bodies or move them?" questioned Sanchez.

"I touched their heads and neck just to see if they were alive, but I realized they were gone."

The families gathered in the room were sullen, but no one was crying. The air was heavy with grief and shock.

Sanchez continued, "Do you know how Amos and Lydia got here? What time it was? Where were they coming from?"

Abram Zook spoke this time. "They were at a youth gathering at the Fisher home. They probably left there around midnight and were going to drop Lydia off before Amos would come home."

"Where is the Fisher home and what is your address Mr. Zook?"

"The Fisher's live on Paradise Lane. It would take about a half hour to get here in a buggy. Our farm is on White Oak Road which is half an hour's ride south of here."

"Did you hear gunshots from your house?" Sanchez asked.

The Beiler's said that they had not, but several of the older teenagers who were in the group said they that heard something that night, but not close to their farm.

"If Amos and Lydia were not shot here, how did the buggy end up on your driveway?" Sanchez wondered out loud.

"Our horses know where they live and can make it home on their own. Amos' horse knew to return to Lydia's home because that was the normal route. But because Amos did not direct the horse to leave and go home, she just stood here until morning."

Sanchez continued with his questions. "Do you have any idea who would do this? Is there anyone that is angry with Amos or Lydia? Were they involved with anyone who would want to hurt them?"

"No," Mervin and Abram said, speaking at the same time.

The Chief put a hand on Sanchez's arm, signaling that he had asked enough questions. Then he said to the group, "Again, we are so sorry for your loss. We will be back to ask more questions, discuss our next steps, and set a schedule for your funerals. Right now, I think we should talk to the other youth that were at the fellowship last night." The Chief and Sanchez both stood and left the families to bear their grief.

When outside, Sanchez asked the Chief why he had ended the questions so quickly. "This happened between the youth gathering and the farm," Miller explained. "The family was in bed; they have no idea what happened. We need to talk to the other youth that were at the gathering and to any of them that were traveling on the same roads as Amos and Lydia."

Sanchez then took the chance to ask the obvious. "You speak Pennsylvania Dutch?"

"I was born into an Amish family," the Chief replied. I'm not totally fluent but I can get by. The Amish appreciate when I speak their language."

"This is like working in a foreign country. I feel really lost. Thanks for helping out," Sanchez responded.

Miller nodded as they walked together to a group of youth that were standing in the yard.

The Chief spoke loud enough for everyone to hear: "Everyone who was at the Fisher's last night needs to meet us there at noon. Please let the others know. What has happened is terrible, but we will get through it." Miller hugged one girl who was crying and in Dutch said, "I am so sorry. We are all hurting."

Sanchez and Miller turned and walked back to the buggy. The bodies had been taken away and only the blood from the two victims remained. The detectives gathered around and Miller drew a map from the Fisher farm to the Beiler farm. "It is a two mile trip from one to the other. The Fishers live at 2505 Paradise Lane, over here." He pointed on the map. "They would have traveled west on Paradise Lane, turned left on Bunker Hill, and right onto Deiter. We will find out later who else was at the gathering, and where they were at the approximate time of the shooting. My guess is that it happened between here and Bunker Road. This road is not heavily traveled and is wide open."

"Do we have any idea of the type of gun used – pistol or long?" Sanchez asked.

Detective Thompson spoke up. "It was most likely a high-powered rifle. There are exit wounds on both victims;. Straight through the chest."

"OK. Start here and walk to Bunker Hill Road," Sanchez said. "Look for any signs of where the gunman was. Look for shells, foot prints, blood splatter, etc."

The detective replied, "It's going to be hard to look for forensics. There have been Amish walking along that road already."

Sanchez replied, "See what you can find. Even if we can't find the bullets or casings, there should be blood splatter and a trail of drops on the road."

The detectives set out to scan the road, shoulders and fields for any signs of the shooting. They noticed some drops of blood on the road where it had leaked out of the floor of the buggy. Those spots were photographed and the road marked appropriately. They reached the rock outcropping and trees and the detectives noticed foot prints. But they could not find any empty bullet shells. The blood spots stopped for nearly one hundred feet and then suddenly they saw blood splattered along the road in a sprayed out fashion.

Detective Thompson said, "This must be where they were shot. There are two fans of blood spray next to each other. It means that the two were virtually shot at the same time. I'm going to guess the trajectory of the bullets was from an upper angle, because the shooter had to miss hitting the horse. That would land the bullets somewhere in that field. The shooter was most likely standing on the rocks over there. The drops didn't show up for a hundred feet because at first, the blood was pooling on the buggy floor. As the horse kept moving, the blood began to drip out of the drainage holes. But it seems that the shooter was far enough away that the gun shots didn't spook the horse. There is no evidence that it ran out of control."

Detective Amaro then asked, "What was the weather like last night? Was there a full moon? It has to be dark out here at night and there are no street lights. I wonder how the shooter was able to see well enough to hit dead on?"

"Don't know," replied Thompson. "If the moon wasn't bright, he had to either use night vision or a laser point or both. If he was familiar with this rock outcropping and knew that Amish kids travel out here at night, he must know the area fairly well."

Amaro wondered, "Is there any reason to try to search for bullets in the field?"

"We'll bring someone out with a metal detector, but those bullets are going to be hard to find, Thompson responded. "But there are more unanswered questions," he continued. "Where did the shooter escape to and how did he leave? Did he have a car, and if he did, where was it? There are tire tracks here, but there are also a lot of different footprints from people walking by. There certainly isn't anywhere close to walk unless you hike up that hill," Thompson said as he pointed to the hill across the road. They noticed that it was covered with trees and shrubs and would not be easy to hike at night.

Amaro had an idea. "If there were two involved, a driver could have stopped and picked the shooter up."

"Possible," agreed Thompson. "I doubt that he would have escaped in a buggy."

"This is what we still do," said Amaro. "Starting from here, we will spread out in a radius and talk with each neighbor to see what we can find out. I feel like this was done by someone close to the community, not by a stranger," he concluded.

Visitors to Amish country are surprised to learn that Amish youth stay out into the early morning hours. It is common to hear the sound of buggies carrying Amish teenagers who are out having a good time with friends. Buggies make an eerie sound in the quiet of the night. The metal wheels on the pavement can vibrate and cause a rumble inside houses that are close to the street.

Chief Miller was in his early 60s, in fairly good shape for his age and had gray, thinning hair. He had lived in Strasburg his entire life. His parents were Amish and, at a young age, left the church when his father made the choice to use rubber on his farm equipment wheels. Rather than abide by the Bishop's rules, he took his family out of the church. They had progressed through conservative Mennonite churches and now Miller attended a non-denominational, charismatic church that had a large number of former Amish and Mennonite members. He had never personally embraced the nonviolent beliefs of the Anabaptist faith and chose to worship God in another way. After graduating from high school he went into the army and served two years as military police during the Vietnam War era. Chief Miller and his wife were the parents of four grown children and had ten grandchildren. One of his sons was killed while serving in the army in Afghanistan.

Because of Miller's background and family ties, he was able to connect with the plain sects of Amish and discuss issues that the State Police normally have difficulty with. It is not that the Amish do not respect the State Police; they just appreciate dealing with someone they know and trust. The Chief was therefore asked to lead a task force for the county District Attorney whenever there was a sensitive issue to be handled involving the plain community.

As the Chief of Police, Harold Miller had oversight of four part-time officers that watched over the Borough of Strasburg from six o'clock in the morning until 2 a.m. Strasburg had never been a violent town. The job of the police officers mostly involved handling traffic citations, domestic disputes, minor robberies and assisting volunteer fire and ambulance departments.

The borough of Strasburg, located eleven miles southeast of Lancaster City, Pennsylvania and sixty miles west of Philadelphia, is an historic town that dates back to the 1600s. The railroad that was built in the nineteenth century continues to be an attraction today.

Although only three thousand residents live in the town, it is a busy tourist spot for people wanting to see the Amish, ride on the old railroad and shop at the nearby outlet stores. Until recent years, it had only one traffic light. It now has three lights and a 'bypass' that directs traffic around the town. Handling the traffic is one of the biggest problems for the police. The posted speed limit through town is twenty-five miles per hour but drivers are always pushing that limit. Second to the speeders is the problem of disorderly conduct around the one bar in town and the bowling alley. Even the Amish youth contribute to the issues and cause problems late at night around the bowling alley and mini market that is open twenty-four hours a day.

Amish youth get into trouble just like any other juveniles. They like to hang out late at night — which surprises many visitors to the area. Alcohol is a big problem with some youth, and in recent years, drugs have entered the community as well. Past arrests made big headlines in the news when Amish youth were caught in a drug raid. Pornography has increased significantly with the access to smart phones and the internet. While the local police cannot say they have a big problem with the Amish youth, they do say that they encounter a greater lack of respect from this generation than those in the past.

When there are legal issues with the Amish, the police use the courts and jail, if necessary. The Chief has the option of going through the court system or turning a young person over to his or her parents and the church Bishop. He often finds that discipline within the church is the best option. The youth face harsh discipline but remain in their community rather than mixing in with other criminal elements in jail. Even with the temptations to become worldlier, most Amish youth have a strong desire to remain a part of their community. When they are removed from the community, they lose their support, traditions, friends and sometimes their family. It can be a hard, lonely experience and some have a long, difficult journey when they have to start over in the English community. When a teenager is asked if they will join the church, they will typically reply, "Of course, I will. Don't believe what you see on those TV shows."

In his thirty years in office, Chief Miller had overseen three arson cases, 300 robberies, multiple assaults — but no murders. Now with a double murder on his hands, he was at a total loss as to why anyone would kill these two innocent young people. Was there something going on with this group of youth that he didn't know about? Was it a random act of violence? Could it have been merely an angry incidence of road rage? And if it was road rage, why would it happen on a back road at night with no traffic? He could understand drivers being frustrated with buggies, but would they be frustrated enough to murder?

Family farming was the main occupation of the Amish until the 1960s. Rising real estate prices and the costs involved in farming have driven many out of the business or forced them to move to less expensive land areas. In recent years, less than 10 percent of Amish households earn their primary income from farming. Many have a combined income of farming and market stands where they sell produce. Other income is derived from employment in wood product production, quilts, greenhouses, bakeries and construction.

At twelve in the afternoon Chief Miller and Detective Sanchez pulled up to the Fisher's home at 2505 Paradise Lane. Sanchez was surprised that the Fisher's did not have a farm, but a simple brick ranch house with a small barn in the back for the horse and buggy. Detective Amaro pulled in behind the buggy that was parked in its place.

Sanchez commented, "So I guess the Fishers aren't farmers."

"Not all Amish are farmers," Amaro explained. "Many of them work in trades like construction and farmer's markets. Stephen Fisher owns a roofing company."

The two men walked into the house where a very solemn group of twenty teenagers and young adults were gathered. The youth sat and stood in a large living room that was designed for their church to meet. Miller introduced himself and Sanchez and then expressed condolences for the loss of Lydia and Amos.

Sanchez began the meeting. "I know this is very hard for all of you. We cannot give many details of our investigation at this time. All we know is that Lydia and Amos were shot and killed sometime after leaving here last night and Lydia's father found their bodies this morning at Lydia's home. What we want to know is if any of you know of anyone who may have wanted to hurt them. Did anything happen last night or recently that could have provoked this? We need details about who was here last night and what time everyone left."

John Fisher spoke up first, obviously agitated. "You don't think any of us had anything to do with this, do you?"

Miller said, "No, John. We are getting the details on who was here and when they went home. We know there were at least three buggies that were traveling around the same time as Amos and Lydia. We're just trying to find out if anyone saw or heard anything."

Reuben King spoke up. "Most of us left here around midnight. I was following Amos on Bunker Hill Road and Jonas Zook was behind me. Samuel, Ruth and Anna Mae were in my buggy and Rachel was riding with Jonas." Reuben pointed to the different young people as he said their names.

"Please write down your full names, addresses and phone numbers on this tablet," Detective Amaro said as he handed a tablet to the closest person. "And write down when you left and who you were traveling with, also."

Reuben continued. "The three buggies were traveling together on Bunker Hill Road. We were laughing and yelling to each other. Amos turned on Lydia's road to take her home. I continued on Bunker Hill to drop off Samuel and Ruth at their house. Anna Mae is my sister. We went farther on Bunker Hill, and then turned onto Saw Mill Road. When we reached home, we went inside." Jonas added, "I am Amos' younger brother. When I left Fischer's, I traveled on Bunker Hill, turned right onto Stively Road and dropped off Rachel. Then I turned on Weaver Road and went home."

"Did any of you see or hear anything when you were on the road?" Sanchez asked. "Did any of you hear gunshots?"

Reuben and Jonas looked at each other and Reuben replied. "Before Amos and Lydia turned off Bunker Hill, a loud truck passed us. The driver was yelling and threw bottles at us."

"Has this happened to you before?" asked Sanchez.

"Yes. There have been some other times when drivers gave us trouble, but we have had a lot of trouble with this particular truck lately."

"Can you describe the truck?"

Jonas spoke up this time. "It's an old Chevy and it's really loud and has big tires. There is a flag in the rear window."

"What kind of flag?"

"Red with a cross. I think maybe it's a Confederate flag from the south?"

"What color is the truck?" Jonas paused, "I'm not really sure. Mostly gray but there are different colors on it."

Chief Miller entered the conversation. "I know the truck and the driver. It is an old truck with body work done on it. It has a Confederate flag in the window. It's owned by Jesse Rutt who lives in the old mill on Spring Road."

Sanchez asked, "Did the truck turn onto Deiter Road?"

None of them knew for sure.

Sanchez asked his last question, "Did any of you hear the gun shots?"

They all replied, "No."

"Right after Deiter Road, Bunker Hill winds up and over a big hill," Reuben explained. "It is thick with trees and then goes down and winds to the right. Sounds can be tricky and don't always carry over the hill. We were also still talking and laughing and Jonas had loud music playing in his buggy."

Reality TV shows have recently crossed over into the Amish lifestyle. The shows portray Amish youth as rebellious and leaving the faith. Dramatic re-enactments were not true and the shows were considered "religious bigotry" by many including Pennsylvania's Governor. Amish youth were portrayed as wild and wanting to leave the boring lifestyle of their parents. Even though Amish do not evangelize or recruit others to join their faith the church continues to grow at a fast speed.

A real life bizarre crime that seemed like a reality show instead of real life was and incident that happened on October 4, 2011. A group of Amish men attacked a forty six year old Bishop in Ohio, dragged him outside of his house and cut his beard. This attack and other similar attacks (some included cutting the hair of women) were charged as hate crimes and the defendants were sentenced to fifteen years in federal prison. Untrimmed beards are more than just a sign of marriage and show great importance and identity. Amish women never cut their hair and it too is a symbol of maturity. The defendants testified that the beard and hair cutting were to bring attention to those who were not living the simple life as God instructed. To add to the bizarre nature of the crime, the leader of the group making the attacks is named Samuel Mullet Sr.

Jonas blushed at that comment, but he didn't disagree.

As requested, each of the young people gave their names, addresses, phone numbers and the routes that they used to go home. All of them lived within a couple miles but none of them had heard gunfire after they left. Sanchez was surprised that everyone had a cell phone, but didn't react visibly.

The detectives thanked the youth for their information and stood to leave.

Two miles south of Strasburg, Creek Road winds beside a small stream on one side and a steep wooded hill on the other. It is not a heavily traveled road because it doesn't really go anywhere. Sections of the road are paved; some are stone and the rest are some kind of blend of the two. There are no shoulders, and if two cars are passing each other, they need to stop and slowly maneuver around each other. The road is two miles long and connects Bunker Hill Road with Weaver Road which is another windy road surrounded by farms.

As the road nears Weaver Road it makes a sharp turn to the right going part way up a wooded hill before making a sharp left and going back down again to open farm land. Tucked into the woods where the road turns stands an old stone mill that has not been functioning for decades. From a distance it looks vacant and ready to fall down.

The stone walls are covered with graffiti and the windows broken out and boarded up. The mill wheel is gone and a small stagnant pond is all that is left from the forgotten operation. A few abandoned cars sit on the property along with a dilapidated barn and two small sheds. The trees are growing so thick around the mill that even on a sunny day in the summer it is dark under the canopy of leaves. At night, it is pitch black. There are no immediate neighbors, but during the winter an old single-wide trailer can be seen up on the hill directly above the mill.

The mill has a long reputation with different generations. To some it is known as Hatchet Man's, and to others, it is called Hell's Funnel. It has been a haven for partiers and Halloween fright nights for generations. The non-traveled road and hidden mill in the woods provide a perfect spot for teens to hide and party. The mill is not visible from any passing road and there are no nearby neighbors who would hear any noise. The mill has become more and more vandalized over the years and the legends grow of the old man who comes out at night and chases offenders away with a hatchet — thus the name Hatchet Man's that has grown in folklore.

Jacob Rutt was a miserable old man who lived alone in a make-shift apartment in the mill. He seemed to fit the folklore ghost of the Hell's Funnel days and soon became known as the current Hatchet Man. He inherited the mill from his parents and made it his home after his wife and son left him. The mill was long silent from its milling years and was heavily damaged by weather, vandals and lack of upkeep. The atmosphere of the place fit Rutt's personality perfectly.

His apartment took up most of the first floor with a flimsy door that led out to rickety wooden steps. Most of the windows in the mill were boarded up with the glass broken out by vandals over the years. There remained three partial windows for the apartment. One was in the kitchen near the door, one in the living room and one in the bathroom. All three windows had wire mesh over them so vandals couldn't knock them out. Old drapes and blinds kept anyone from seeing in or out. The apartment was dark, damp and dirty. The roof had leaked for years and water ran down the walls. It was drafty when the wind blew and always cold in the winter. It was heated by a wood stove that was surely not up to code. There was no air conditioning. The kitchen was bare with a twenty-inch propane stove, a small refrigerator from the 1960s, two metal cabinets and an old cast iron sink that had been white before the enamel wore off. The floors throughout were wide pine planks with no rugs. Exposed wires added to the fire hazard and so few of the lights worked that it was consistently dark inside.

Although Jacob was rumored to be Hatchet Man, there were never any charges brought against him for hurting anyone. He was known for chasing partiers and young couples parking along the gravel road. He chased off teens that drank beer and littered his property, and ghost hunters that were trying to video a ghost sighting. Now in his seventies, he was partially retired from a roofing career, and he kept to himself in the mill. He rarely left the property and only went out occasionally for groceries and beer. Social Security paid his light bill, property taxes and food. He heated the apartment with wood that he cut down around the property.

Jacob's heavy drinking and erratic behavior had led his wife and young son Jesse to leave him. They moved to Charlotte, North Carolina to live with her grandparents. Even though Jesse didn't grow up with his father, he somehow picked up his traits. His drinking habit started before he was a teenager, and by his teens would fight anyone who crossed his path. He was no stranger to the local authorities. His mom kicked him out of the house at age eighteen and he shacked up with anyone who would take him.

In his mid-twenties, Jesse met Susan Myer who was a bartender at the local bar. They moved in together and became the new domestic dispute home for the local police. Jesse worked in construction but was constantly changing jobs. Construction jobs are daytime jobs and bartenders typically work at night. Having the two on opposite schedules had both benefits and drawbacks for the couple. It helped keep them apart most days, but it also led Jesse to feel jealous and suspicious when Susan was at work.

One night after Jesse drank his limit, he drove to the bar where his wife was working and found her in the parking lot with a customer. Jesse was enraged. He nearly killed the man with his bare hands and decided he better leave town for good before getting arrested. With no money and nowhere else to go, he returned to the old mill. That was the last time he saw Susan and the first time in years that he saw his father. He wasn't sure which one was worse: living in jail or living in the old mill again with Jacob.

Accidents between buggies and cars or trucks can be traumatic and deadly. Buggies offer very little protection when hit. Sometimes accidents are fatal to the passengers but in almost every accident, the horse must be put down. Horses can also cause tremendous damage to a car when they collide.

Jesse drove an old 1984 Chevy pickup that still had unregistered North Carolina tags on it. The actual color of the truck could not be identified. Between mismatched body parts that were covered with primer and rust, it wasn't easy to tell what was original and what was replaced. The truck sat high with large tires. The muffler was blown, so it could be heard coming from as far as half a mile away. Besides the noise, the only other characteristic that made it stand out was the Confederate flag covering the back window.

When Jesse moved to Lancaster County, he was able to pick up another construction job in the area. When he wasn't working, he was at a bar, trying to avoid the mill and drown away his problems.

The one thing that Jesse didn't leave behind in North Carolina was his temper. He was angry about living with his father again in the old mill. He was angry that his life was in shambles. He was angry that he didn't have any money. The old version of the "Old Hatchet Man" stories quickly changed to "Young Hatchet Man: the psycho with a shot gun that would shoot anyone trespassing on the property." The police were called on occasion but little was done because no one was ever hurt. Jesse would shoot in the air to get the kids, and so-called ghost hunters, to leave.

The problems began to spread when Jesse let his anger explode on the road. He didn't like the summer tourist traffic around Strasburg, or the Amish buggies that they came to see. Tourists are known to drive slowly and follow the buggies, trying to take pictures. Jesse often complained: "Who in the world wants a picture of an Amish buggy and a corn field, anyway?"

Amish buggies in Lancaster County are gray and black with a black steel frame. The wheels are wooden and have a steel rim that runs on the road. There is a door on both sides and a lift window in the back. A bench seat is in the front for a driver and passenger and there are side bench seats in the back. Buggies are equipped with twelve-volt batteries that supply power to head lights, flashing lights and windshield wipers. This standard buggy will carry an entire family. Buggies can be decorated with some variations of lights and reflectors as long as they meet the Bishop's approval. There are variations to the standard buggy. Some have an open-bed for carrying material. Buggies are made locally and need to be ordered in advance. At times, there can be a year-long wait for a new buggy.

Amish boys learn to harness a horse and drive buggies at a young age. Boys will be given their first buggy at age fourteen or fifteen. Most Amish girls learn to harness a horse and drive a buggy but they don't often own their own. A family may own several buggies one for the family, a two-seat open carriage and possibly an open wagon. The courting buggy is a two-seat open carriage with a bench seat. Since they are open, there is very little privacy to hide any inappropriate behavior. Although these buggies are made for two people, it is not uncommon to see four or more youth piling in and sitting either on top of each other or backwards facing the driver. All buggies are required to have battery-operated lights, turn signals and a fluorescent triangle sign on the back.

The Strasburg police had heard complaints from a few tourists and locals about road rage incidents involving an old pickup truck. But most of these happened out of the Strasburg borough limits, where the local police did not have jurisdiction. Rather than call the State Police, the locals tried to convince the Chief to talk to Jesse, which he did, often without any success.

## Tuesday, June 16th

The headline in the local newspaper read "Amish teens killed in Strasburg." The article gave limited details about the killings of Amos Zook and Lydia Beiler. There was a picture of an open buggy and of the Beiler farm. There were eight interviews with neighbors including Mr. and Mrs. Leaman who testified that they heard the gunshots at half past midnight. The local TV stations had their reporters around the area filming the back roads and also the town of Strasburg. The Philadelphia news stations had not yet picked up on the story. Amish do not allow their photos to be taken but there were some Amish who were willing to speak to the reporters off camera. One neighbor said that they heard tires squealing around that time, but weren't sure if it had anything to do with this incident or not. Everyone was in shock and questioned "why" to a senseless killing.

The Chief, Detective Sanchez and two other detectives met at the Strasburg Police Station at 8:00 a.m. to discuss the case. They had to push reporters back from the entrance of the small station while several TV cameras filmed their movements. Inside the office they each grabbed a cup of coffee and sat down around a table with a map of the area. Two of the local officers were there and after introductions they stood nearby listening to the conversation. Sanchez started the meeting with a summary of the previous day's events and a report from the medical examiner.

The Chief spoke next. Pointing to the map, he said, "Here is the borough of Strasburg and the road where the killing happened." He took a sharpie and marked the two areas. "The kids were at this house and here are the locations where each one traveled that night." He marked several roads on the map with sticky notes with names on them. He also marked off the locations of the other teen's homes.

"We have walked the road several times and ran a metal detector over the area but we haven't found any bullet fragments yet," Detective Amaro said.

"Yeah it will be a miracle to find a bullet in that area," added Sanchez. "They may have hit the pavement and ricocheted anywhere in the field. Do you officers have any information from people in town?"

"No information," reported Officer Duncan, "just shock. No one knows anything about these two. We've never had any trouble with them or their youth group."

Sanchez explained, "We didn't see any evidence of drinking or drugs. Toxicology tests will be done but it doesn't appear that there was any inappropriate behavior."

"I know this group of kids," Officer Ward said. "They aren't that type. They are good kids and I doubt any of them are involved with substance abuse."

"That may be true, but we still need to check," insisted Sanchez. "Teenagers are teenagers no matter what, and they may have gotten into something that no one was aware of."

The Chief shook his head, "I highly doubt anything like that. I agree with Ward. This is a good group of kids and we have never had any problems with them. We need to check all the possibilities but let's keep looking for something else that would have led to this shooting."

Sanchez said, "So, we know where they were shot and we will finalize forensics on the buggy and road area. We know who was at the party and where they were all going. We know the time that it happened. What we don't have is motive. Why were these two picked out and killed?" He paused as everyone contemplated what was before them.

"We have one lead — a guy with an old truck that likes to harass the Amish when he drives by. The Chief and I will be visiting him today. Amaro and Thompson, continue to canvas the shooting area and talk to both families again to see if they have any more information. Ward and Duncan, I want you to keep talking with town people. We will meet back here at 3:30 this afternoon for updates."

They all left the room and battled out through the media again with Sanchez telling the press that they would be given an update at five o'clock in the evening.

Church and family relationships are very important among the Amish. Schooling takes place in one-roomed, Amish schools, and most children walk to school. If the children live too far away, the local school districts offer busing. School education ends at the completion of eighth grade, after which children begin working on the farm or in other Amish-owned businesses.

A buggy pulled up the drive and Reuben and Fannie Zook climbed out. Reuben tied the horse to a hitching post. They wore black clothes and walked stoically to the kitchen door without speaking to any of the children. Ida met them at the door and invited them in. Mervin joined them and the four sat down at the kitchen table where they had met with the police the day before. The propane lantern was still burning to give light to the room. There was no emotion as they talked in their native dialect of Pennsylvania Dutch.

Customs are passed down from generation to generation. This includes funeral traditions. Amish believe that when a person has died, they are no longer on earth and that they have gone to live with God, in heaven. In their funerals, they don't focus on the person who has died or past memories. Instead, they focus on God and the eternal life that waits for them. Funerals are normally in the family's home and usually within a short time of the death. Some Amish do not embalm the corpse, which means that they are required to bury within three days.

Since the police were holding the bodies of Amos and Lydia for tests and autopsies, the families would have no choice but to embalm and use the services of a funeral home.

The Beilers and Zooks were in the same church community and that community would help organize the funerals, meals, build a coffin and do the burial. As the families talked, two more buggies came onto the property and two men and two women approached. They were two elders from their church along with their wives. Their discussion focused on the funeral plans, not on the loss and pain that they all felt. It was better for them to work through details and not to focus on their tragedy. Throughout the day, buggies came and went. Food was delivered to both families. Friends came to help with the farm work and chores.

Although Amish have experienced some discrimination over time, most have lived peacefully with their English neighbors. During the World Wars, there was some anger against those who refused to help with the military effort. Most current day frustration is caused by traffic issues with buggies. In areas with heavy traffic, passing buggies is dangerous and can cause traffic to back up. Drivers have been charged with throwing rocks, bottles or trash at buggies. It is not uncommon for young drivers to hurl obscenities or drive too close to the horse and buggy which can cause serious injury or death if contact is made. This anger is not against the Amish religion but is due to frustration on the road; it is similar to how some drivers harass bicyclists.

The Chief and Sanchez pulled up the gravel drive off Creek Road and approached the old mill. The Chief knocked on the flimsy door fearing that it would break. Stray cats, some clearly in need of a vet and looking starved, watched them from the weeds. The door opened and Jacob Rutt stood in bare feet, torn work pants, a filthy "wife-beater shirt," several weeks of stubble and greasy, thin hair. He was missing several teeth but since he didn't smile, Sanchez would not have known.

"Morning, Jacob," said the Chief.

"What brings you out to Hatchet Man's?" asked Jacob.

"Jacob, this is Detective Sanchez from the State Police. We want to talk to Jesse. Is he around?"

"He's at work. Won't be home until five unless he stops at the bar again. Lately it's been more like seven when he gets back. What do you want with'm?" Jacob leaned forward and spit a wad of chew on the ground and wiped his mouth with the back of his hand.

"Just want to talk with him about some complaints from the Amish about his driving," Chief Miller said, trying not to raise any alarm.

Jacob pointed to Sanchez, "This guy speak or is he just along for the ride?" Sanchez crossed his arms and stared at the medieval man before him. "I don't know anything about Jesse botherin' Amish kids. I'll let him know you stopped."

Sanchez replied, "You don't need to tell him anything. We'll be back."

Jacob spit again almost hitting Sanchez' shoes and closed the door.

Sanchez turned and walked back to the police cruiser in disgust at this man, the filth of the old mill and the sick animals around it. When the Chief caught, Sanchez asked him, "What the hell is this place? I feel like we are in a hollow in Appalachia."

"They are quite the pair," Chief offered. "Jacob lived here for years since his wife and son left him. He made the first floor into a makeshift apartment although it would never pass any building codes. His entire existence can fit in a bottle. From what I hear, Jesse isn't too far behind his old man. He moved down south with his mom when he was a kid. They couldn't take Jacob's drinking and erratic behavior. I don't know when he came back or why. I've gotten a few complaints about his driving but we've never been able to catch him in the act. Still, I don't think he would go to the extent of murder."

Sanchez replied, "I'm not so sure. I've seen a lot of violence over road rage. If that old coot can drive, I wouldn't put it past him, either."

They drove back to Strasburg where Sanchez dropped the Chief off at his office. He drove on to his office at the State Police Headquarters to do some research and background checks on the Rutts.

A driver near New Holland, Pennsylvania shot and killed a horse pulling a buggy carrying Mr. and Mrs. Stoltzfoos and their four children. Mr. Stoltzfoos told the police he had no idea who the driver was or why he would do something like that. The State Police arrested the driver: Ted Manning, a twenty year old with a long record who claimed he shot the horse for absolutely no reason. It had just occurred to him and he did it. He pled to animal cruelty, unlawful use of a firearm and carrying a weapon without a permit. He was made to pay restitution and sentenced to five years in State Prison.

Whatever knowledge Chief Miller lacked regarding murder investigations, Detective Sanchez made up with first-hand experience. They balanced each other out with Amish experience and murder investigation. They also had a good chemistry and worked well together. Sanchez was forty-five years old and had lived in Philadelphia before moving sixty miles west to Lancaster County. He had started out as a beat cop and moved up to a homicide investigator in his thirties. His wife of ten years left him due to his crazy work schedule. After reflecting over his life, Sanchez decided a change was necessary. He applied with the State Police and transferred to the country six months before this incident. Sanchez was raised in a Spanish Catholic Church and while he didn't struggle with the murder side of this case, he was lost with the traditions, language, culture and beliefs of the Amish. The Chief filled him in on Amish traditions as they worked together.

A man was arrested in Quarryville for trying to give Amish teenagers beer at a local convenience store. He drove off but then returned to the horse and buggy and stopped suddenly. The horse ran into his vehicle. He showed them his gun and yelled, "Rumspringa!" No one was seriously injured but the horse had minor injuries. The police chased and arrested him for supplying alcohol to minors and carrying a gun without a permit. He was sentenced to a year of probation and community service.

Sanchez sat back in his office chair reading through this case and the information they had so far. Who would kill anyone in this peaceful community and why? Was this a simple case of road rage or an attack on a lifestyle? Could these kids have gotten into something way over their heads — like drugs? Sanchez had heard rumors of wild parties with Amish kids. He had seen the TV shows reflecting bizarre behavior and rebellion. Could there be some truth to that and could the violence of the big city be coming to this community? If it was drug related, the situation was only going to get worse.

In 1998 two Amish men were indicted on charges of buying drugs from the Pagan motorcycle gang and selling them at dances in Lancaster County. "Bikes and buggies, it's strange," State Trooper Dickens said. "Our investigations are leading to problems that we never dreamed of years ago." The attorney representing the Amish said, "The pressures of modern society and temptations affect everyone." Their attorney also stated that the two men still plan to join the church after their "rumspringa" is over.

Sanchez wrote down some things that we wanted to follow up with Miller: Had Lydia Beiler been in any other dating relationships? Could jealousy have been a part of the problem? Have any of the local Amish kids gotten messed up in drugs? Toxicology report — were they drinking at the time or were drugs in their systems? If they were dealing in drugs, could this be a deal gone bad or revenge for not paying?

Rumspringa is Pennsylvania Dutch for "running around." Young people between the ages of sixteen and twenty-one have freedom to behave in ways that may not be accepted after they are baptized in the church. Some Amish teens will own and drive cars during this period but most will also continue using a horse and buggy. Rumors of rebellious behavior, wild parties, drinking, and drug activity exist. Most adults don't acknowledge the wild behavior and justify this time as a necessity before settling down into the plain life. To some it is a rite of passage. Amish youth may wear non-traditional clothing and hair styles but it is frowned upon at home. They may leave their homes in their traditional dress and change clothes at another location before going out. Youth will often travel, see movies and associate with English teens.

On October 2, 2006 a lone gunman suffering from depression overtook an Amish school at Nickel Mines, Pennsylvania, killing five Amish girls and injuring another five. The girls were between the ages of six and thirteen years. As State Police surrounded the school, the gunman took his own life. He was a milk truck driver who knew many of these children and their families. News of the shooting went quickly through the community — both English and Amish. Local news crews were immediately on the scene and national media picked up the story. Reporters, photographers and news crews descended on this rural area that is several miles from Strasburg and the story was reported around the world. Although the Amish wanted no publicity or attention, this incident could not avoid drawing worldwide attention.

The story covered the front page of the Lancaster County newspapers. While the Amish mourned for their children, the entire community grieved with them in shock. First responders were traumatized. People of all faiths gathered for prayer services in local churches. One Amish man said, "Today, we are all Amish." Fundraisers raised money for the Amish families, and donations came in for the shooter's wife and three children. These donations exceeded four million dollars in total. The immediate and total forgiveness shown by the families inspired books and movies about the event and touched people around the world.

Most road rage situations occur in the moment of heated interaction, and not later as a planned revenge. It didn't seem that a road rage incident would have erupted on that road at that hour of the night. Would Rutt really stage a murder as payback for his rage?

Sanchez looked over reports that had been pulled on all the characters involved. Amos and Lydia had no prior record, which he expected. Jacob Rutt was also clean. Jesse Rutt, on the other hand, was not. He had open arrest warrants from Charlotte for aggravated assault, terroristic threats and attempted murder.

That was enough to warrant taking action. Sanchez picked up the phone and called Charlotte for more information.

The officer on the line warned Sanchez, "He's got a hot temper so be careful". He also said he would be grateful if Jesse could be extradited back to North Carolina if he wasn't guilty in Pennsylvania.

Sanchez wasn't taking any chances with this guy. He was the number one suspect at this point. Even if he didn't kill these kids, he needed to return to Charlotte to face other charges. He wasn't going to take any chances with an explosive suspect who had a history of drinking and violence. He placed a call to his commander to provide these details.

In response a Special Emergency Response Team (SERT) was assembled and met to look over the situation. The Lieutenant in charge reviewed the map of the area and discussed options for the best capture of Rutt. There were only two ways in to the mill, and they didn't want him to be able to escape into the woods. It was decided that the four-man team would be positioned in the woods with sites on the mill to wait for Rutt to come home from work. Each man was camouflaged and carried assault rifles and pistols except for one who had a twelve-gauge shotgun. The team informed Sanchez when they were in place and the waiting began.

Following the Amish school shooting, the world openly responded to the reaction of the Amish families that lost their children. When the families offered forgiveness to the killer's family, those outside the plain community were in shock. Most people admired this and made the goal to be more forgiving in their own situations. But others criticized the forgiveness and how the Amish responded. Some believed that evil needs to be combated through vengeance. Everyone was angry at this senseless killing and wanted punishment. When the Amish forgave, they were challenged with a reaction that they were not prepared to handle. Could they really forgive the person who killed their child?

Back at the Strasburg Police Station, Sanchez informed the media that the five o'clock update would be postponed but did not share any details. He went inside and gave Miller the update. It was now four-thirty and Jacob had said his son could reach home as early as five. At five-fifteen the SERT Lieutenant called Sanchez, "He just pulled in. His description matches what the Amish kids said — an old Chevy truck with primer and mixed color panels. He's inside the mill."

"Ok," said Sanchez, "We'll be there in five minutes. Don't let him leave."

"How do you want to handle bringing him out?" Miller asked as they drove to the mill.

"I've been debating that. I don't want to expose either of us to danger, but I don't want him to get scared and barricade himself in either. At this point, he just thinks we're talking about harassing some Amish kids with his bad driving."

"Let me go to the door," said Miller, "Let's not make this explode into something that it's not."

"But how do we know what it is and what it is not? What if this guy really is a killer?" wondered Sanchez.

"We'll find out soon enough. I'll stand back from the door and your guys will have clean shots, if necessary."

They pulled into the drive at the mill. The SERT team was well hidden even the Chief could not see them.

Sanchez radioed the team and told them the plan. Two of the men had clear shots at the door. Chief Miller walked up to the door, knocked and yelled, "Jesse, it's Chief Miller. We need to talk."

Jesse yelled out without opening the door, "What do you want this time Miller? I wasn't even at the bar today. I just came home from work."

Miller said, "Jesse we need to talk about a complaint on your driving and harassment of Amish buggies."

Jesse finally opened the door. "What's going on, Miller? What did I do wrong this time?"

"Just come out, Jesse. Detective Sanchez is here from the State Police and we need to talk."

The door opened a bit wider and Jesse stepped outside and came down the steps to the Chief. A younger version of his dad, he had long hair that needed to be washed, a scruffy beard, an old t-shirt, work pants and boots. A cigarette was hanging from his lip. "What does a State cop want to talk to me about?"

Sanchez approached Jesse and spoke into a microphone, "C'mon on in." Two of the SERT members came around the corner with guns pointed. The other two with sites on Rutt stayed in place.

Rutt was in shock as Sanchez stepped behind him, put on handcuffs, and said "Jesse Rutt, you are under arrest."

"What's this all about, Miller? I didn't do anything except scare a couple Amish kids." The other two SERT officers came in and Jesse was patted down. At this point Jacob was at the door growling at everyone; Miller told him to shut up. One of the SERT officers ordered him outside.

Sanchez said to both men, "Jesse you are under arrest for charges outstanding in Charlotte, North Carolina and you are a suspect for the murder of Amos Zook and Lydia Beiler."

"Amos who?" Jesse snapped, "Miller, what is he talking about?"

Jacob yelled, "Murder? He didn't kill anyone." He began to approach Sanchez until one of the SERT officers stepped in and blocked him.

Sanchez said, "We have a search warrant for all the buildings on the property and the vehicles. Detectives will be here shortly."

Jesse was read his rights and put in a cruiser. Four detectives pulled on to the property. Three of them began searching the mill while one began asking Jacob questions. Jacob didn't want to cooperate until the detective suggested that the interrogation could be done at the station if he didn't want to do it here.

As they talked outside, the detectives went through each building and vehicle. They found two 12-gauge shotguns, one hunting rifle and one 38-caliber Smith and Wesson pistol. They were bagged and removed from the property. The rifle was a possible match for the weapon that killed Amos and Lydia.

Jacob reported that he knew nothing about the Amish kids that were killed. He said Jesse had come home Sunday night around 11:00 p.m. and fell asleep on the sofa. He couldn't swear that Jesse didn't go out at midnight, but he never heard him all night. He insisted that Jesse was "no murderer".

The Amish church communities are divided geographically. In Strasburg there are four church districts. Churches meet in homes instead of in church buildings and services are held every other Sunday. Church groups can be up to 150 people in each district. Each church owns a wagon that carries backless benches for people to sit on and this wagon moves from house to house where needed. Amish men and women sit apart from each other. Hymns are sung and scripture read in Pennsylvania Dutch. There are usually three to five preachers and one Bishop in each district. Following a church service, a meal is served for everyone.

Two detectives questioned Jesse at the station but got nowhere fast. Rutt claimed he was home sometime around eleven and that he didn't go out again until 6:30 a.m. for work. He didn't know anything about those Amish kids and he would never kill anyone. By 8:00 p.m. the detectives put him in a holding cell for the night.

The autopsies on Amos and Lydia were completed by Wednesday morning and although the full toxicology reports wouldn't be ready for weeks, the District Attorney released the bodies since it seemed clear that Amos and Lydia died from the gunshot wounds and that any other foul play was unlikely. The autopsies revealed no other markings on the bodies. There were no signs of struggle. The bodies were transported to a funeral home in Strasburg where they were embalmed and prepared for the families. The Beilers and Zooks agreed to have the funeral ceremonies together in the Beiler home on the following Tuesday. Their families and church community were notified and everyone came together to plan the all-day event. Neighbors would help with necessary farm chores. There was concern over media attention and people outside their community trying to get near the home. The State and Strasburg Police along with the Fire Police agreed to help with traffic control and they closed off Deiter Road at the nearest intersections. Only Amish buggies and people with close family connections were permitted on the road.

Funerals, like many practices, vary from church to church but they all reflect the core values of community, humility and simplicity. The entire community helps the grieving family with chores, food and work for the funeral. If finances are needed, the families in the church will contribute until the need is met.

Sanchez began Wednesday with the DA and detectives working on the case. Without the bullets to match Rutt's gun they would not be able to prove that he was the shooter. There were no witnesses and no proof that he was on Dieter Road that night. Since there was no hard evidence to hold Jesse on a murder charge, they charged him with being a fugitive from justice and transferred him to authorities in Charlotte to serve his time on previous charges. At the same time, authorities in Lancaster continued investigating the recent murders.

After the transport plans and arrangements were made, Sanchez drove around the Strasburg area again trying to see if they could have missed something. Driving down Bunker Hill Road, he got behind three buggies in a row while going up the windy hill. There was no visibility. He may have been able to pass one buggy, but not three. He began to understand some of the frustration that drivers experienced. "Why do they bunch up together?" he said out loud for no one to hear. The line of cars grew longer and longer behind him as they all crawled at five miles an hour over the hill.

Sanchez stopped at the site of the shooting. He climbed the rocks to see the shot line. He looked at the fields around him. Where did the shooter park? There was no room to pull off the road. Did he just stop on the road? That would have been possible, since the road had very little traffic, especially at that hour of the night. If his vehicle was blocking the road, how did the horse and buggy get around it? How did he see them clearly enough for two clean shots? Sanchez looked over the reports and notes. Most of the neighbors were interviewed within a half mile radius, but no one had any additional information. Most homes in this area were scattered and not close to anyone. The other issue was the time of night. Most of these residents were already sleeping.

As he scanned the view from up on the rocks, Sanchez noticed that it really was a beautiful area — rolling fields and hills covered with trees. It was so peaceful, and yet horrible murders happened right in this spot. Sanchez heard an animal move on the wooded hill behind him. As he turned and looked to see what it was, he noticed for the first time something that looked like a trail through the woods.

He crossed the road and started walking up the hill. There was a rough trail — one that had not been cleaned out for a long time but obviously still a trail. Footprints were visible, so they had to be recent. He continued up to the top of the hill where other trails seemed to cross and go out in different directions. He followed each one, seeing tree stands in trees for hunters. Most of the trails were short and didn't go far. One trail continued to an open space that was cut out of the trees. It was flat and open. On the other side of the space the trail continued and went down the other side of the hill. He saw an old single wide trailer with a small barn. Below the trailer he could see part of the old mill where the Rutts live. By walking this trail, Jesse could have easily walked over to Deiter Road.

Leaving the church before baptism is criticized but not condemned. But an adult who has been baptized in the church will be shunned if he leaves. Non-Amish family members may sit at a different table for meals and experience other signals of their non-belonging. These are indicators of separation.

Tuesday was a beautiful day and buggies began lining both sides of the road at seven o'clock in the morning. Friends and family wore all black clothing and walked quietly to the home. Volunteers agreed to help with the horses and tied them to ropes between trees. Many of the family members were driven to the house by Amish taxis. Visitors gathered outside the home waiting to go through a viewing line. The funeral home had dressed Amos and Lydia in traditional, long, new, clothes. Amos wore a white vest and white shirt while Lydia wore a long, white dress with an apron. This would have been her wedding dress in the fall. Neither had any makeup and they were in simple handmade wooden caskets with their upper bodies exposed for viewing.

The caskets were side-by-side in the living room of the house. All the furniture was moved out so people could move through more easily. A line formed and visitors moved solemnly through the house until early afternoon. Benches had been brought inside and the two-hour funeral service began. Using only Pennsylvania Dutch, the service began with the creation story from the Bible and continued on to include additional scripture reading and thanksgiving to God. There were no flowers, no singing and no eulogy for the two that died.

Chief Miller and his wife attended the funeral. They were friends with these families and they understood the Amish customs. The Chief was there to mourn with the others, not as the police chief. Even so, as a policeman, he stayed inquisitive and alert. He knew that most if not all of the family and friends, but there was one man who stood out as a stranger. He was dressed in Amish attire, about thirty years old and without a beard, which meant that he was single. He seemed to be alone and not very familiar with the families.

Miller made sure he had a chance to speak with this man after the service. He introduced himself as Aaron King and explained that had he recently moved into the area from Ohio. He was living in a trailer on top of the hill near the old mill. He didn't have family here but was hoping to settle down in the area. He was working for Strasburg Roofing.

King explained that he had heard about the shooting and wanted to support the families. Miller offered to introduce him to some people but King was a little backward about it. Not backward, really. He seemed nervous.

The Chief commented to him, "King. That is a common name around here. Are you related to any families in Lancaster?"

"No, my family live mostly in Ohio and a few are in Indiana."

"What town are you from?" Miller asked him.

"Millersburg," was the answer. "But I left there about ten years ago and have lived in a few different counties."

Then Aaron turned the questions to Miller. "You're not Amish? Are you friends of the family?"

"My family was Amish when I was born but left soon after," Miller said. He decided not to reveal that he was Chief of Police in town.

"It's not easy leaving the church. It's hard to make friends and fit in," King commented

"Are you still a part of the church in Ohio?"

"No," he said.

Miller kept pressing in. "Will you be joining the church here?" he asked.

"I'm not sure," stated King.

As they spoke, King became more and more agitated. He obviously didn't like all the questions and he made an excuse to walk away.

Miller then asked Benuel Lapp, one of the Amish Bishops, "Do you know that man named Aaron King? He just moved here from Ohio."

Benuel replied, "No, I'm not familiar with him. He is not part of our fellowship."

"Please check with the other leaders and see if anyone knows him. I will talk to you tomorrow. I am sorry for your loss."

At the end of the service, men carried the caskets outside to two wagons that were ready and waiting. The horse drawn wagons carried Amos and Lydia to an Amish cemetery one mile away. Friends had prepared the sites by hand-digging graves. The mourners followed the wagons to the cemetery and gathered to have a final viewing and prayer before lowering the bodies with ropes into the graves. The Lord's Prayer was spoken and a final prayer shared before leaving. Many of the family returned to the home for a shared dinner. It was understood that the families would return later to place simple tombstones at the graves stating the deceased names, birth dates and death dates.

On a hill in the distance, local and Philadelphia news crews tried to film as much of the proceedings as they could. A helicopter flew overhead with a photographer getting pictures and film from above. No photographers or reporters were permitted near the house or cemetery, but they still found a way to snap photos.

That evening, the local news carried the story showing the buggies lining the road and families walking toward the farm. The news also showed a picture of Jesse Rutt and reported that he was being held for suspicion of murdering Amos Zook and Lydia Beiler.

Amish children go to school only through eighth grade, so at the age of fourteen or fifteen they are working full time, either for the family business or another Amish employer. While Amish girls learn early to harness the horses and drive buggies, they generally don't own their own buggies unless they remain unmarried. Young woman receive trousseaus of dishes, linens and furniture, instead.

Wednesday morning was gloomy and rain fell throughout the day. The gloom matched the mood of everyone related to this case. The funeral and burial services were over and everything was cleaned up with the exception of the bench wagon that was still sitting on the driveway. Amish families were back to their daily chores. Very little was said about the funeral or loss to the families. Jesse Rutt was held for the standard forty-eight hours and then transported to Charlotte to face his charges there. The police hoped that they could gather enough proof for indictment while he served his time for the earlier charges.

Jacob Rutt woke and shuffled around the dirty apartment like he did every morning. He hadn't visited Jesse during his two days in the local prison and he didn't call anyone for updates. He didn't care. Bitterness was about the only way to describe him. While some had bad times and moved on, Rutt's life had seemed like one disaster after another. The old mill was a good reflection of the old man – broken down with no apparent purpose.

With a mug of coffee in his hand, Jacob walked up the stairs to the second floor of the old mill. In a corner, boxes were stacked with junk that no one wanted. The police had gone through them but when they did, it was obvious that the contents hadn't been touched in years, so they didn't dig down into them. Jacob moved some of the boxes and exposed several wide floor boards that were not nailed down.

Amish women wear plain-cut dresses in solid colors. Aprons can be worn at home. Unwed women wear white aprons, while married women wear dark colors like purple or black. Triangular pieces of cloth called capes are worn in the teenage years and are pinned to the aprons. Women can often be identified in the community by the types of prayer coverings that they wear. Prayer coverings vary in size, shape, color and the presence or absence of strings hanging from the sides for tying. Their hair is never cut but is either braided or pulled into a bun. Some women lose their hair at the part from pulling it so tightly for so many years.

Men wear dark-colored trousers that are held up with suspenders. No belts are worn. Straw hats are worn for work or as casual attire. Black felt hats are worn on Sundays and for other formal events. Shirts can be any bright, but solid, color. Men often wear boots and younger men will wear black sneakers. Single men keep their faces shaven. Once married, men will grow untrimmed beards. Mustaches are forbidden and shaved even when beards are grown. Men's hair is cut (some would say chopped) by women in the house. Young men and boys often have thick blonde hair that is bluntly cut, straight around the head near the ear, in what locals call a "bowl cut."

Lifting the planks, he pulled out a rifle, shot gun and pistol. He had hid these on Monday afternoon after the first visit by Miller and Sanchez. Now that they had searched everywhere and taken Jesse, he wanted the weapons available in case he needed them. He put the floor boards back down, shoved the boxes back and kicked the dirt around to cover his hiding place.

Sanchez finished his morning duties at the State Police station, grabbed Detectives Amaro and Thompson and journeyed to Strasburg to meet with the Chief. The four sat around a large table drinking coffee. The map of the area was still on the wall, along with pictures of Amos and Lydia. The new face on the wall was Jesse Rutt.

Miller explained, "The funeral and burial went as planned yesterday. Everything was quiet and the media didn't try to disturb anyone. We had told them they would be arrested if they tried to get close. I met a single Amish man there who didn't seem to belong."

Sanchez asked, "Why? What was wrong with him?"

"He didn't know anyone there. Says he just moved into the area from Ohio and hasn't been a part of the church here yet. He is about thirty and he's not married."

"Something wrong with that?"

D rug abuse has had an impact on the Amish communities. Although it has not been rampant, there have been problems. In three communities there are reports of illegal activity and actions that the communities are taking:

MILLERSBURG, Ohio – Over 100 Amish filled a barn for a meeting about Methamphetamine and other drugs affecting their community. Holmes and Wayne counties are about 90 miles south of Cleveland and although illegal drugs have not been a big problem in the area, authorities are concerned with evidence of it creeping into the community. Holmes and Wayne are home to Ohio's largest Amish community.

NAPPANEE, Indiana – It may be the last place you think of drug abuse but the Indiana State Police are attempting to get the word out about the dangers of drugs and alcohol abuse.

ARCOLA, Illinois – A hotline center has been established for the Amish in need of drug and alcohol counseling. Authorities have been notifying the plain sect of a confidential center where they can talk with counselors and medical personnel about their issues.

"No, not necessarily. But it is very odd for a single man to move to a whole new community and not join in right away. If he is not in fellowship with these families and doesn't know them, why was he at the funeral? He clearly didn't know anyone, and was nervous and fidgety."

"Do you know anything else about him?" asked Sanchez.

"Says he works for Strasburg Roofing," Miller replied. Then he called Officer Singer in and told him to check with the Roofing Company. "I'm going to talk with the Bishops this morning and see if they have any other information about him."

Sanchez replied, "Ok. Let's keep that in mind and keep working on the Rutt's and other neighbors to see if they know anything new. I have to say that funeral was quite the experience. I have never seen anything like that. The row of buggies lining the road was amazing. They showed no anger or bitterness. It was so peaceful. Just amazing."

Amaro and Thompson both agreed.

"Many of the Amish are asking whether or not it is safe to go out in their buggies," Officer Singer said. They want to know if we have the killer." Over the last week the Amish had avoided going out at night in their buggies and used Amish taxis instead.

Sanchez answered, "That's a good question. I'm still betting on Rutt and he is locked up. We don't want to mislead them, but we also don't want them to shut their doors and stay inside forever."

"I'm not as confident. I wouldn't want my kids out in a buggy at night right now," said Miller.

"Do you think we have the wrong guy?" asked Sanchez.

"Not necessarily. I just want to be sure."

Amaro said, "We can patrol more in this area, but there are so many back roads. We certainly can't protect them all."

Sanchez stood and walked over to the map, looking closely at the pins. "We'll have extra patrols in this area," he said, waving his hand over most of the Strasburg region. "Miller, I have a question," he continued. "I went to the murder site yesterday, and I found a trail that goes up this hill. At the top there was a flat field and a bunch of other trails."

"That field is an old runway for a plane. A man lived in a house near there and he used that field to land and take off. He died a few years ago and now it is farmed."

"But the trail continues on the other side and goes down to the old mill," Sanchez added.

"Are you thinking that Rutt walked over the hill on the trail, killed the kids, and then walked back?"

"It crossed my mind. I saw an old trailer up there in the woods. What do you know about that?"

"That's the other thing that is bothering me about this Aaron King," said Miller. "He says he is living in that trailer. Those trails are used by local hunters. Mostly for archery hunting. They sit up in those tree stands. I know the owner has rented that trailer out from time to time but it is really old and getting run down."

"I looked around but didn't see anyone. I didn't see any evidence of a horse and buggy. If this guy is Amish, wouldn't he have a horse and buggy?"

"Maybe. That doesn't bother me as much as the location of the trailer near the mill and that it is up the hill from the murder scene. I wonder if he is friends with Rutt or if he has any more information on what happened that night." said Miller.

Sanchez barked, "I don't believe in coincidence. The fact that this guy shows up in the community from another Amish town and is living near our suspect and the murder victims is a little too suspicious. Maybe this guy and Rutt did this together after drinking all night. I want an APB on Aaron King, and I want a search warrant for his trailer. I don't want any of this leaking out. For now, I think the families should keep their kids off the road at night. Miller and I are going to run out and talk to the Bishops."

When an Amish member does not uphold the community expectation and cannot be convinced to repent, he or she will be excommunicated and may be shunned. Shunning is the practice of limiting social contacts in hopes of shaming the wayward person back to the church. The severity of the shunning varies depending on the family, community and the nature of the local church. The violation will also determine how severe the punishment is and how long it lasts. A violation in some communities may be as minor as using rubber tires on a wagon.

Shunning and judgment depend a great deal on whether an individual joins the church or not. If an individual does not get baptized and does not take a church vow, that person will not be held to the standards of the church. They may be separated from others but not fully shunned. However, once an individual is baptized and joins the church, the decision is for life. Leaving the church is a severe offense. Almost all Amish teenagers choose to be baptized and join the church.

Everyone left the conference room with instructions. Officer Singer went to Strasburg Roofing. Amaro and Thompson ran background searches on King and called for a search warrant for the trailer. Sanchez and Miller headed out to visit with several Amish leaders. Once they were in the car, Miller said, "Lancaster County has had forty unsolved murders since 1992. I hope this isn't another one."

"Not on my watch, Miller," said Sanchez with determination.

Chief Miller and Sanchez met with the Bishops of the three Amish churches around Strasburg. They all had questions about the murders and whether it was safe to go out at night in their buggies.

"The man we have arrested may be involved, but we don't know for sure yet. He is serving time for prior arrests in North Carolina. We are checking on another man, too. His name is Aaron King, and I met him at the funeral and talked to Benuel about him. Do any of you know him?"

After discussing the question among themselves, the men agreed that they didn't know him. They wondered why he had come to the funeral if he was not related to anyone.

"That's what I am trying to understand. He was dressed Amish and says that he recently moved here from Ohio, but he is single and drives a car. He works for Strasburg Roofing. He said he has made acquaintances at church, but something didn't seem right about him. He lives in the trailer on top of the hill near the old mill."

"How old of a man is he?"

"I would guess about thirty. Have any of you met him?"

Levi Fisher spoke up, "Aw, yes. I did meet a man fitting that description. I forgot his name. He came here from the Amish community in Ohio, but I don't believe he was ever baptized. He was dressed English and driving a car when I met him. Why do you think he has a part in this?"

In the Amish community almost everyone now carries a cell phone. It's not just the kids anymore. They have access to 911 and can report problems. They also have access to the internet and are able to take pictures with their phones. Alcohol has always been a problem with Amish teens, but the biggest problem affecting the whole culture now is pornography. Since everyone has a phone and internet, they also have access to pornography. Porn addictions are affecting the culture and families where sex issues have historically been hidden.

Miller said, "I would rather not comment on that now. I'm just checking him out. I thought it was odd that he would come to the funeral if he doesn't know any of you." The men agreed and they would talk to other family members who had connections in Ohio.

"I would tell your young people to stay off the roads until we have this figured out. Thank you for taking the time to meet with us," concluded Sanchez.

Officer Singer stopped at Strasburg Roofing and talked with the owner, Marlin Smoker. Smoker was a big man with hands that practically crushed anyone who dared shake them. His family owned several construction companies that did roofing, siding and window replacement. He knew everyone in the area and everyone in the construction business.

"I hired King a couple months ago. He moved here from Ohio. Has Amish background out there," said Smoker as he handed King's file to Singer.

"Did you run any background checks or talk to references?" Singer asked.

"No, and no. I hire these guys, and I can tell in a day if they can handle the work. He is a good worker and I can tell he has experience."

"Any trouble with him?"

Local police are reporting a new level of disrespect from Amish youth. There is a great deal of anger, resentment and rebellion toward anyone in authority. It is a big change from any generation in the past. In regards to legal issues, often the family and church deal with problems better than the courts would, and at least help the youth stay out of jail.

"Not on the job," said Smoker, "but he hooked up with that Rutt guy, Jesse. Jesse works for my brother, and he is trouble. Those two met on a job and began drinking together at the bar in Strasburg. I don't think either of them will last here very long. Rutt is in jail and I doubt he will be coming back. King started acting really strange after the murders and he hasn't shown up for work the last two days."

"Chief said he was at the funeral yesterday."

"Really? He's not part of the church, and I doubt that he is friends with any of them. He complains about his Amish background all the time. Says he moved here to get away from them. His family kicked him out before he joined the church because he was drinking and using drugs. I think he served time out there. He doesn't have one good thing to say about the plain community," Smoker concluded, scratching his head. He looked baffled.

"Why move to Strasburg if you want to get away from Amish?" wondered Singer.

"Exactly my point."

"You said he was acting strange since the murders. How so?"

Smoker thought a second, "Hard to describe. Just strange. Nervous and not focused. Agitated. He kept looking around like he was looking for someone and not concentrating on his work. When his supervisor said something, King began yelling at him and walked off the job."

"Thanks," said Singer. Let me know if he shows up. "Can I take a copy of his paperwork?"

Singer went back to the station and began searching for records of King in Ohio. His first call was to the police in Walnut Creek in the middle of Holmes County. They sent a long report describing an Amish young person who got into drugs and alcohol in his teens and was arrested for minor charges. He was in and out of county detention, but his behavior had been getting worse instead of better. Singer talked to the Chief of Police, Richard Denlinger and found that King had become violent and was also arrested for a number of thefts.

"King is a troubled soul," Denlinger reported. "If I had a psychology degree, I would say he has a number of mental health issues – bipolar to begin with. He began drinking as a teen and experimented with drugs and then got into trouble in other ways. His family thinks his behavior can be blamed on the devil and drugs. They are not interested in hearing anything about mental disorders. According to them, the problems all stem from the sin in his life," said the Chief.

"Did he ever get any help with the substance abuse or mental issues?" asked Singer.

"No. We tried disciplining him in the church the first few times and that didn't work. He beat up one of the elders who was trying to help him. We tried jail. That didn't work. We tried rehab and counseling and that didn't work either."

"So what happened?"

"His family and the church finally kicked him out and stopped all relationships with him. They sort of shunned him, or at least told him to leave. Even though he hadn't joined the church they felt that he had turned his heart against God. They would have welcomed him back if his behavior changed, but that never happened."

"Without his family and the church, he was totally on his own. He began moving around a lot, staying in cheap motels and doing odd construction jobs. Sometimes he was okay but after awhile he would act out again. Like I said, to me he had a mental condition that needed to be treated. I lost track of him a few years ago and I heard he moved to Indiana or Illinois. His family hasn't heard from him either. He is one troubled guy."

Now Singer had to find out more. He did searches in Ohio, Indiana and Illinois. He searched for Aaron King and also general Amish crimes. The searches turned out to be frightening and he quickly called his Chief to report.

Amaro and Thompson came to the gravel driveway for King's trailer and drove up the bumpy path to an old, faded, green, single-wide trailer. The roof must have leaked at some point because roofing tar dripped down the sides of the trailer. Old sheets and newspaper covered the windows and it didn't look like there was electricity or any other services. A small barn and an outhouse were in the back. They knocked on the door, but no one answered.

Psychiatrists have found that shunning and ostracism have harmful effects. People who are ostracized suffer deeply; this manifests in depression and many other physiological symptoms. This experience causes a loss of self-esteem and a loss of feeling valued. A person's sense of community or belonging is also lost. Shunning is a social "cut off" similar to being placed in solitary confinement in prison. The most outstanding result is rage.

Thompson was digging through the trash next to the door. "Sanchez is right about someone living here," he said. "There are food containers with current dates on them." The door was closed with a small padlock. Thompson picked up a nearby rock and broke the lock off. "It amazes me that people don't lock their doors up here, he commented."

Amaro checked the surrounding property, looking for anything that looked out of place. He checked inside the shed but it was empty. There was also an outhouse in the back. Thompson and Singer entered the trailer. They found some food in the kitchen and clothes on the floor. There was no electricity, but a propane lantern sat on the counter. There were papers on the bed and a paystub from Strasburg Roofing in the name of Aaron King. Digging through a pile of clothes, Amaro found a box with 9-mm bullets. "Well, well, look at these," he said. They finished their inspection and went back to the station, calling Sanchez with the information.

The team met back at the Strasburg station, and each reported what they found. Each report was damning on its own, but put together, it was a nightmare.

According to experts, drugs do not lead to mental illness and mental illness does not necessarily lead to drug abuse. However, the behaviors in both situations can be similar. Mental illness often surfaces in the late teens or early twenties. That is also the time when many people experiment with drugs. Mental illness can lead someone to use drugs, but neither one causes the other. Drug abuse only heightens the symptoms of mental illness. It is a bad combination.

Singer told about his searches through the Amish communities in various states. King got out of county prison in June 2013 and went off the grid. His Amish community wouldn't take him back, and his growing behavior problems made it hard for him to hold down a job. "I was able to track down a few jobs that he had, but he didn't leave a very big trail. Here's where it gets scary: In July of '14, there was a tragic hit and run in Holmes County; three Amish girls were killed and one was severely injured. The cops never nailed anyone for it."

Sanchez questioned, "Do they think it was King?"

"They didn't at the time. He was in Indiana at that point. They thought it was just a crazy driver that beat them to the charge. There were no eye witnesses to the vehicle.

Then in January of 2015, a sixteen-year-old Amish boy was found beaten and strangled in Indiana – again, no suspects and no clues or links to King but the authorities did not doubt that he might have been involved. That June, two Amish girls, sixteen years of age, were abducted in Illinois. They were beaten pretty bad and found days later wandering in a field forty miles from home."

Sanchez said, "Let me guess... no suspect?"

"Right. All these crimes happened to Amish teens between sixteen and eighteen in strong Amish communities. I bet that if we had time to interview families and cheap motels in those communities, a single man fitting King's description would be named."

Detective Thompson commented, "And no one ever put this puzzle together, because they were so unrelated with different MO's. The only linking factor was that they were all Amish teen victims in random crimes. So, did King come to Lancaster County to attack another Amish community?"

Sanchez replied, "I think there's a good chance of that. He also became friends with Rutt. Maybe Rutt got involved, but King looks like a sure bet. We don't have time to follow up on any more of this now. The perpetrator who did these other crimes left the community after he was done and moved on. We need to get King now before he flees to another area."

The Amish have been criticized for how they handle some violations of the law. In 2009, an Amish group in Missouri faced charges for failing to report a known child abuse issue. Amish do not have a belief against reporting crime, but because they value privacy, there are cases of abuse that are never reported. One man said it this way, "All men fight sin and temptation, and they want to keep it hidden. Amish men are no different. It is easy to think these peaceful people don't struggle with sin, but they certainly do."

It was early evening before the team put all this together and, by that point, a group of Amish kids had left to see fireworks for the fourth of July. They hadn't gotten the message from the Bishops, and assumed that it would be safe to go out since Jesse Rutt was in prison. It was a six-mile drive from the fireworks to their homes, and twelve kids piled on top of a wagon.

When the fireworks ended at 10:00 p.m., the group pulled out of the parking lot. They didn't notice a black car parked near them or the man who was watching them. They headed back to Strasburg. Three miles of the journey were on a main road which was busy and backed-up with traffic from the local live theater that had ended around the same time. The black car followed them for some time before passing. When they got to Strasburg, Chief Miller saw them and pulled them over.

"Why are you kids out here tonight? I told your leaders that you should stay off the roads," he scolded.

Isaac Stolzfoos was driving the wagon and said, "I'm sorry Chief. We didn't hear that. We left home this afternoon to have a picnic and then went to the fireworks. We're just now going home."

Miller looked at all the kids in the wagon. He knew all of them and shook his head. "I can't let you go on, but I'd need a bus to get all of you home. How many of you are piled in here? Move over. I'll drive." He was imitating a Terminator movie but the kids didn't get it. He gave a nudge to Isaac to slide over. "I'll take you home, and one of my officers will pick me up." Leaving his cruiser in town he climbed up on the seat with Isaac and began the journey on Bunker Hill Road. They dropped off the first set of siblings and continued on. They wound their way up and over the hill and made the ninety degree turn back into the farm land. It was a dark night with little light, and Miller felt a chill go through him as he realized how defenseless they were.

A car was headed toward them and as it approached, the high beams were turned directly on the wagon. The car stopped, blocking the road, and the Chief pulled back on the reigns of the horse to stop. He pulled out his service revolver and keyed in his radio mic, "Chief Miller, Strasburg Police, Bunker Hill and Creek Road, possible suspect, Aaron King. Requesting backup."

He told all the kids to get down in the wagon and stay quiet. He whispered to Isaac, "If there is any trouble, get the kids into the field to hide." He stood to jump off the wagon as the driver of the car got out and fired two shots at Miller. The horse reared up in panic as the gun fired, and Miller fell to the ground. In the back of the wagon, the kids were screaming. Isaac shouted to them to jump out and run into the field of tobacco plants and hide. He grabbed two of the smaller ones who were frozen in fear. They ran into the tall, tobacco plants and fell down flat while bullets flew around them. There were screams of pain as someone was shot.

Miller hit the ground violently and rolled to the side of the road away from the panicked horse and wagon. The shooter continued to fire in the location where he thought Miller was. He shot and killed the horse who was about to jump right onto his vehicle that was blocking the road. With Miller on the ground not moving, he began moving in the direction of the tobacco field where he saw the kids run. He was firing aimlessly into the field.

Lying on the ground gathering his senses, Miller saw King moving towards the kids. King had left his lights on and now he was the one exposed to the light. Miller shot at him and King fired back before stumbling back to his car. Miller continued firing at the car as it pulled away on Creek Road. He pushed his radio mic, "Officer down....." as he went unconscious.

Sirens were coming from every direction. As the police arrived at the scene, they found the dead horse, the empty wagon and Miller lying on the road. They didn't see any kids, and they were trying to figure out what happened. Officer Singer approached, knowing that Miller was helping kids who had been in the wagon. He called for an ambulance as other officers attended to Miller. He pointed his spot light on the tobacco field and told the kids it was safe to come out.

Isaac was hit in the arm, and his friend Anna Mary was shot in the leg. The others appeared to be okay except for cuts and minor injuries from jumping out of the wagon and into the field.

Miller came to. He was wearing a vest but had been hit once with a bullet that penetrated around his shoulder. Between the shots and the impact of falling from the wagon, he was going to be sore for several days. The first ambulance arrived and more were called. In addition to the bullet wounds, he broke his arm when he fell. They loaded him into the ambulance. A second ambulance showed up and the EMTs began treating the twelve kids and took preliminary care of the bullet injuries. The kids were all transported to the hospital in ambulances and police cruisers.

Sanchez and his detectives arrived as Miller was being loaded in the ambulance.

Sanchez said, "Miller, you okay?"

Miller responded, "Yeah, just trying to be Amish again." The ambulance door closed, and they headed to the hospital.

King was shot, and he was bleeding badly. He turned on Creek Road and drove back in the direction of the old mill. Sirens were blaring from all directions, and he knew he had to get off the main road. He thought if he got back on the Amish roads behind the mill, he could hide.

As he approached the turns around the mill, the blood loss was causing him to swerve. He passed out and drove into a rock along the bottom of the hill where he had been living. He came to and stumbled out of his car onto the gravel drive.

A voice called out, "Who's out there? What's going on?"

King got to his feet and stumbled forward. "Jacob, it's me, Aaron King."

"What are you doing, King? What are all the sirens?" Jacob Rutt was walking toward King with a shot gun pointed at him.

"I think more Amish kids were shot," said King still staggering toward Rutt.

"What's wrong with you? You're bleeding. Are you the one who killed those kids?"

"You wouldn't understand. You have family. I don't have anyone. My family kicked me out!"

"You caused my son to get arrested and blamed for what you did," Jacob shouted."

King raised his arm and pointed his gun at Rutt. "None of you understand."

Rutt did not wait more than a second. He fired his shot gun and sent King flying backwards from the blast. "No, we don't," said Rutt, "and we never will."

Police cruisers were screaming down Creek Road and the troopers jumped out with weapons drawn, yelling at Rutt to drop his weapon. He dropped the shot gun and raised his hands. A trooper ran to him and picked up the shot gun. The others went to check on King. He was dead. They picked up his gun and checked for ammo. It was empty.

******************

Sanchez drove into the hospital and checked on Chief Miller. "How are you feeling?" he asked with a weary voice and tired eyes.

"Like I was shot and fell off a wagon. I'm too old for this kind of action. I'm supposed to be living in the quiet, peaceful town of Strasburg."

"Yeah, and I was supposed to leave Philadelphia for an easy ride in Lancaster County."

Both men were quiet as they reflected on the events of the last two weeks.

"I think it's over," said Sanchez.

"Yeah, I think it is," agreed Miller.

## Morning News Conference, Strasburg Police Station

Detective Sanchez reported on the events of the previous night and opened the floor for questions from the media.

"Is it true that Aaron King was killed by Jacob Rutt, the father of Jesse Rutt, the first suspect in the Amish killings?"

"Mr. Rutt shot and killed Mr. King in self-defense on his property. Mr. King had already been shot by Chief Miller, and we believe that those previous shots would have been fatal whether Mr. Rutt shot him or not. King was bleeding out and nearly unconscious while driving, which led him to run into a rock. He then exited his vehicle with his weapon drawn."

"Will there be charges filed against Mr. Rutt?"

"No," Sanchez explained. His actions were in self-defense. Mr. King was approaching Mr. Rutt with a hand gun."

"The report on Mr. King said that he was a drug abuser and suffered from mental illness. Can you elaborate on any of that? Is it true that Mr. King was Amish?"

"Mr. King was raised Amish in Ohio. He experimented with drugs as a teenager and was arrested several times for drug-related activity. His mental illness, which was never clinically diagnosed, seemed apparent to local law enforcement agencies and the community, but we have no proof. Mr. King did not join the church, so he wasn't officially shunned. He was cut off from his family because of his behavior and unwillingness to abide by the rules."

"Could his mental illness have been caused by the drugs he was taking?"

"From what I know of drug use and mental illness, drug use does not cause mental illness."

"Was Chief Miller really driving the wagon when King attacked them?"

"Yes. The Chief didn't want the kids going out in the country alone, and he couldn't fit them into his cruiser, so he drove the wagon."

"What is the status of the children?"

"One was shot in the arm and one shot in the leg. There were some minor injuries from jumping out of the wagon and running into the field but nothing serious. We expect full recovery of all the youth."

"Will this clear Jesse and Jacob Rutt from any other charges?"

"They may face some harassment charges but yes, they will likely be cleared of all murder charges related to this case unless we find some connection between them and King."

"Do you think the shunning or excommunication caused King to act out this way?"

"Let me say that this family should not be blamed for what has happened. The traditions of the Amish faith have been long-standing and affective. Few of the Amish members stray from their faith and even fewer get into legal trouble. However, abandonment by any family is being studied as a form of 'bullying' which leaves the ostracized family member feeling alone and unwanted. We don't know if Mr. King would have continued rebelling and acting out violently if he had close connections with his family. It may have helped him. We will never know."

"We can't blame his family, but he was clearly taking revenge on other Amish kids," one reporter insisted. Their questions seemed relentless.

"We have families that are suffering here, and in other Amish communities, from the alleged acts of one man. Let's keep them in our prayers and hope that they will grow stronger from these tragedies. And let's pray that nothing like this ever happens again. Thank you for coming out today."

## Follow up

Jesse Rutt finished his incarceration in North Carolina and moved back home with his father. By all appearances, it looked like father and son were trying to cooperate with each other and working on repairs around the mill. There were no further reports of Jesse harassing Amish buggies.

Detective Sanchez and Chief Miller continued working together in situations around the county involving the plain community.

The Amish communities in Lancaster, Ohio, Indiana and Illinois were able to find closure for their losses. The topics of shunning, excommunication, discipline and abandonment were not discussed but drug abuse and mental illness were.

On Sunday night Sanchez couldn't sleep. He began thinking about the culture among the Amish: black buggies, gray buggies, scooters, roller blading, can't ride horseback, can ride horseback, can't ride bicycles, buttons and zippers, coverings, dresses, black hats and straw hats — who makes up these rules? He had heard about Amish before, but didn't know that there were so many right ways and wrong ways of doing just about everything.

Rules on clothing, hats, coverings, beards and more. The lifestyle was fascinating to him, even though all the rules and rigidity were overwhelming. The idea of forgiveness and peaceful living really touched him. They were the opposite of what he experienced in his upbringing in the city, and what he encountered everyday in his job. His family was scattered and certainly not close geographically or relationally. What happened between him and his wife?

Wouldn't it be fun to live on a farm with all those children and animals around? Thinking of that helped him understand why so many kids joined the church and skipped the English lifestyle.

As he drifted off to sleep, he thought about the dangers of living in the city compared to living in the country. But then again, riding in a buggy on a dark night in the middle of nowhere didn't seem very safe either.

## Other books by Brian Fulmer

### Children

*The Baobab Tree*

*From My Front Door*

### Non Fiction

*Why I Don't Invest in Real Estate*

*So, You Want to be a Missionary*

## Contact

**Brian's blog** missiontomission.wordpress.com

**Twitter** @brian_missions

**Facebook** Brian.Keith.Fulmer

**Email** missiontomissions@gmail.com

From readers of Brian's other books:

*The Baobab Tree*

"A timeless parable, skillfully illustrated, and filled with extraordinary meaning for persons of any age. Readers learn to notice the abilities and gifts of persons that often are overlooked and denigrated in society. This is a wonderful way to share another world culture, while teaching virtue and honor of those who seem unlike ourselves."

"A lovely, inspiring story!"

"A sweet story that teaches us that even if you're different and can't do what others can do, you still have a purpose and special talents and qualities that others do not have. Well written with beautiful illustrations!"

*Why I Don't Invest in Real Estate*

"This book was spot on for any real estate investor or for anyone considering real estate investment. People for years have been saying the benefits of real estate, but never talk about the associated costs, headaches, and potential disaster to your finances. I would highly recommend this book if you want a no nonsense take on real estate from an expert. Don't get fooled by the get rich quick real estate books and programs, it's not what it seems."

This was a very realistic evaluation of some of the pitfalls of investing in real estate. Brian lists some of the more common issues that people overlook when investing. The true stories were very interesting.

*So You Want To Be A Missionary*

"Brian Fulmer has done an excellent job compiling a pithy, poignant, and sometimes hilarious assortment of real-life, cross-cultural stories that will entertain, inform and sometimes shock you. People really do live differently around this great big globe we all call home. Every person who is planning to travel or live abroad would benefit from this quick tour of the world experienced through the eyes, ears, and taste buds of other intrepid world adventurers. Highly recommended."

—Doug Gehman, President Globe Missions

Coming in 2018: A novel titled *Healing*

Amy Newell was a normal kid going to college and playing field hockey. After being prayed for at a Christian festival, Amy was told that she had the spiritual gift of healing. Christian leaders and the community question if Amy is real or a fake. Accusations and hysteria follow Amy and her family, forcing them into hiding. Are the healings real? Are they demonic? Why is God using a young girl in this way? Why are they angels involved? What will happen to Amy and will she ever find peace in this "gift?"

Follow Brian K. Fulmer on Amazon to learn of a publication date.

48624394R00059

Made in the USA
Middletown, DE
24 September 2017